Dream Visits

Stories for the Inner Child Series

Nothing is Nothing, Book 1, 2013
ISBN-10: 0-944164-24-2

Something is Something, Book 2, 2014
ISBN-13: 978-0-944164-28-0

Dream Visits, Book 3, 2015
ISBN-13: 978-0-944164-30-3

Mother, Book 4 *coming December 2015*

Dream Visits

Steve Gallegos, Ph.D.

Printing History

First Edition

1st printing: May 2015

Cover Artwork: Mary Diggin,
info@marydiggin.com

ISBN 978-0-944164-30-3 (Print)

ISBN 978-0-944164-25-9 (Kindle)

Moon Bear Press
PO Box 468
Velarde NM 87582
orders@moonbearpress.com
www.moonbearpress.com

Contents

Dream of the Village

David could see the village in the distance. He seemed to be flying high above it. Then he realized he was Eagle, surfing on the air. The air was a landscape he could feel, with various layers of density, and he instinctively moved his wings and feathers in order to maintain a position on the surface of the sea of air that supported him. He was amazed at the power of his wings; with a few beats he could climb from one level to another. But even more amazing was the precision of his vision. He could see the village in its entire breadth stretched out between the mountain and the sea, and at the same moment he could see very precisely what the various people below were doing. It was a kind of seeing that he had not known as a human.

He realized that the village seemed much older than he had

remembered it. And suddenly he saw several large ships in the sea, ships with large sails. Many tiny humans were swarming into small rowboats that were traveling back and forth between the ships and the village. As he looked more closely he saw that many of the men were dressed as sailors and had beards. Many of them at the edge of the village carried rifles or swords. He didn't recognize anyone in the village and that surprised him because he had known everyone when he had lived there. A sudden realization jarred him: the village that he saw and the ships and all the people, were several hundred years before his time; he was looking into a scene from the past.

As he looked more precisely he saw that the sailors were not at all interested in the life of the village nor in the particular people that lived there, but they seemed glued to things in the village; they were going around touching some of the carved posts and handling various blankets, and even feeling some of the blankets and clothes and hats as the villagers were wearing them. This intrusiveness was exactly the opposite of the respect that he himself had known in the village. He realized what he was seeing was a meeting of two different kinds of people, of two different cultures, and that what each culture experienced was very different. The sailors had no sense of the depth of feeling in the village culture, and the village people did not initially realize that the sailors were hardened and coarse and saw the world only in terms of acquisition. He knew that the main perspective in the village was a deep respect for aliveness itself but the sailors seemed oblivious to the living people and only looked at things that were lifeless.

With his eagle eyes he saw that the sailors were arrogant and disrespectful toward the villagers, treating them like the goods they were inspecting, and that the villagers, with their natural respect for aliveness, were puzzle and perplexed. At one edge of the village David saw one of the sailors touching a young girl in an aggressive way and showing her his teeth. Her father standing nearby grabbed him and pulled him away. Surprised, the sailor pointed his weapon at the man and fired. Everyone in the village froze as he fell to the ground covered in blood. The two groups faced each other, the sailors with weapons drawn and the villagers not knowing how to respond. The tension seemed to cause the air itself to stand still, and Eagle sailed directly into the crowd. Eagle's claws raked across the face of the man who had fired opening deep cuts. The man dropped his weapon and grabbed at his face with both hands. Every eye was on Eagle and the sailors began a quick retreat to the boats that had carried them to the shore. The entire village knew that Nature had come to protect them and rushed at the sailors, pushing them toward the boats and sending them on their way.

David awoke, panting and sweating, he couldn't seem to breathe deep or fast enough. Opening his eyes he looked around the guest room, relieved to find himself here at his childhood home. But a part of him was still overlooking the village, aware of the conflict, and realizing that he was being called to action. He just didn't know what he was to do.

Clawface

David's dreams continued, night after night. They were similar and different. But always he was Eagle, flying high over the village. He came to regard the dreams as a sort of historical perspective of the life of the village. He wrote them down so he could eventually tell Grandfather about them, and perhaps journey into them himself.

He saw the wooden ships with large sails return for the second time, but now there were many more ships, and the sailor whose face he had raked with his claws was among the men. He had three long scars that ran up each cheek. They had been roughy sewn so that the stitches had also left scars of their own, and David thought they looked like the tracks of a small bird dragging a worm or like fine red carvings. The man had let his beard grow long and bushy to try to hide them but they continued up each cheek, had missed the eyes, and ran for a short way up his forehead. The man looked ferocious and David could see that the men he was with both reviled and feared him.

David wasn't sure whether he had heard his name from the other men or if it just appeared on its own: Clawface!

The men entered the village with a ferociousness and even greater disrespect than he had seen before. Storming into the village they began taking whatever they wished, pushing people aside, and forcing their way into the houses. Eagle saw Clawface searching, looking around for something or someone, and Eagle knew he was looking for the young girl that he had approached so roughly the first time the ships came. Eagle also searched for her with his keen eyesight, and he was relieved to see that she was in the mountains with her father and mother and little brother. They were searching for mushrooms and had already gathered two small baskets of them. Eagle knew they would be bringing them back to share with the entire village.

Eagle also noticed that Clawface regularly looked up into the sky and there was always fear on his face and he flinched when he looked up. Eagle knew he was looking for him. Eagle hoped the sailors would leave before the girl and her family returned from the mountains but he knew that would probably not happen.

The sailors continued to abuse people in the village, slapping some of them and even shooting two of the men who tried to intervene. The girl and her family returning from the mountains with their cache of mushrooms heard the shots and stopped abruptly. They crept quietly toward the village and stopped suddenly before leaving the treeline, seeing the mayhem that was happening in their village. Whispering quietly they understood the danger, were tempted to rush into the village to try to help their friends, but hesitated and thought it wiser to wait and watch, realizing that there was little they could do. Then the father saw Clawface and surged forward, being held back by his wife and two children. They knew that if he entered the village they would all be slaughtered, or worse.

Eagle could only observe from his treetop, but he was relieved that the family remained hidden.

Dreaming

David had learned from Grandfather that there were various types of dreams, and that most dreams were personal dreams, guiding the individual into growing or healing. Other dreams foreshadowed happenings that later occurred. And still other dreams were instructional or transformational dreams meant for mankind in general. But the dreams David was receiving seemed to be indicative of historical times, and that he was experiencing events that had taken place long ago. But he was surprised by the fact that Eagle, through whom he was viewing the events, had even participated in some of them.

But perhaps participation was a way of recognizing his own essence among the people of the village. He realized that he cared deeply for the entire village and everyone in it, and that some sort of action was or would be needed in protection. How does one person protect an entire village?

His dreams left him with many questions and few answers, but they did awaken him to the fact that he felt himself to be more a member of the village than of this home that he had just recently returned to. Except for Cornelia.

His feelings toward Cornelia were complex. He realized she was a sister that he had always missed even though he had just now met her for the first time. He also felt a deeply protective care for her. But there was also this strange mystery, the mystery of a deep wisdom that he recognized in her that didn't seem to have a place within his understanding. How could such a young person have such a powerful way of knowing? Her knowing, her understanding, her wisdom were much deeper and older than she was.

David knew he would have to take her to meet Grandfather.

Jarred

But then David had another dream that jarred him to the core.

He was again looking through the eyes of Eagle. A single ship had arrived in the bay and a lone rowboat had left the ship and was making its way slowly toward the village. The people of the village were all gathered along the shore, some of them armed with clubs and knives and other weapons. David watched as the rowboat crept along the waters surface, bobbing and slowly moving toward the mob of villagers. When it was close to shore Clawface suddenly jumped out of the boat and waded toward the villagers. To David this felt like an act of suicide. Surely they would kill him. As he reached shore the armed villagers gathered around him. His rowing companions remained in the small boat apprehensive about whether they should leave immediately but holding their breath while watching the scene that was unfolding.

No one touched Clawface. There was something about his presence that seemed to surround him with a glow. The crowd parted to let him through and he walked directly up to the father of the young woman with whom he had initially had such an intrusive meeting. David saw him talking and gesturing to the father. The father stood in silence with his daughter, wife and son at his side. Clawface continued to gesture, to plead, to speak more and more rapidly, but David could not make out a word of what he was saying. He then motioned to his companions in the small rowboat and they brought out many blankets and hatchets and tools of various sorts including sharp knives and small glittering objects. Clawface had them lay these at the feet of the father and his daughter. Suddenly David realized that Clawface was bargaining for the companionship of the daughter!

The small family left the objects where they lay and then retreated inland with the rest of the villagers while Clawface and his companions stood by the gifts that they had brought over in the small boat.

David watched as the villagers spoke, one after another, the daughter spoke and her father spoke, then the mother and other villagers and the talk went on and on but always with great respect.

David was aware that he had expected an outright slaughter of Clawface and his companions, but that the villagers were in sincere discussion with each other, and that something very mature was taking place. He then looked closely at the daughter, and realized that there was a soft glow around her very similar to the glow that he had seen around Clawface as he had entered the village. Clawface and his companions sat in a half circle near the gifts he had brought as the villagers conversed.

Suddenly David awoke. It was still dark and he was lying in the guest room. He didn't remember having gone to bed and didn't really even know what day it was but that seemed unimportant. What seemed to have awakened him was a brief shade of a memory of something taking place at the dance in the village, the dance at which he had begun to experience the depth of human presence here on the earth.

He remembered the atmosphere in the large wooden building: the fire, the shadows, his feeling of companionship with the three boys he had just met and eaten a meal with. Then the dancers began to emerge from the shadows. He remembered the wooden masks with the large beaks that clacked as they opened and closed. He realized that there was a distinct rhythm to this wooden clacking and he could see again the rhythm of the movement of the dancers. The rhythmic drumming that had preceded the dancing continued to increase in pace and intensity. He saw that inside of the beaks of the bird masks there was another countenance, a face, sometimes human, sometimes animal. And he experienced again the strange feeling, as of something deepening, of being pulled more deeply into himself, and then of the panorama of faces and events and presences that he felt within himself, something that almost frightened him except for the fact that there was also something deeply comforting about this experience. He realized that he had felt as if he were part of something much larger, much greater, a continuous presence, an aliveness that had not begun with him but of which he was only one of an endless ongoing link. He had felt deeply that he belonged!

And then it suddenly struck him. He had seen a mask and felt a deep shudder throughout his body. The mask was of a human face, and the face had three red lines on each side, on each side of the forehead and down each cheek. These were the scars that Eagle had left on Clawface!

Helpless

For the next few days David felt very strange. Something was happening that didn't make sense. Spirals seemed to be connecting within him. Memories, thoughts, dreams, possibilities. He couldn't sort things out and seemed to be in some sort of daze. Knowing seemed to have escaped its normal bounds and he was frightened. Something didn't make sense and yet there was an experience within himself of deeper layers that had a sense of their own. His own boundaries seemed to be melting and he was unsure of himself, and yet at the same time he felt a certainty of his place in the world like he had never felt before, but it was a place that was deeper than belonging to a human world. He sense that in some strange way he belonged between worlds but he didn't know what those worlds were or how he had gotten here or if he could ever get back. But maybe he didn't want to go back.

He felt he had been living in a place that was narrow and shallow and superficial. A place of surface and uncertainty, but also a place where he played a role of knowing. Yet here he was dancing in an unknown place, reaching for something or some-one that was not available (or perhaps not yet available), yet not knowing what or where he was reaching toward. He was afraid and yet had never felt more certain in his life. The feeling was deeply uncomfortable and exhilarating!

His experience was that several worlds were merging together in ways that were not allowed. And suddenly he real-ized that his own thinking was having difficulty just allowing the experience he was going through. He needed more control but he didn't know how or what to control, or so he thought. He felt his thinking straining itself to make sense of what he had been experiencing. Could dreams in fact have an effect on what happened in the outer world? And could dreams influence things that had already taken place hundreds of years ago?

Then he was aware that he had an investment in the outcome of what he had been dreaming, and that he was taking dreams as reality when perhaps they were only dreams. He understood that he was stepping into a previously unknown way of knowing, and he wanted things to follow a structure that he was comfortable with and in which he felt safe. Was he in fact going crazy? And what was crazy, anyway? Just because he didn't understand and was confused, did that make him crazy? He wanted the world to fall into a structure, a logical structure, but perhaps there was a deeper way things worked that he had not known before. Did this mean he was crazy, or was his own thinking just reorganiz-ing itself on a new level, one that he had not yet arrived at even though he knew he had already left his old level. He felt himself to be in a no-mans-land where there were no signposts that he understood, a place where a new language was being created and he kept trying to use the old language that he had learned since childhood. He felt frustrated and helpless.

And then he suddenly brightened. Wasn't it this exactly? He wanted his frustration to disappear and in order for this to happen he was trying to force his feeling of helplessness to disappear. What if he just accepted being helpless in this new place, admit to feeling helpless and embrace it fully, and allow himself some room for things to change within his understanding! That was it!

So he laid down on the couch and just melted into helplessness, acknowledging that he didn't know what to do, and that not knowing what to do did not mean that he was out of control, but just that he needed to give up trying to control the situation in which he found himself. He felt strange, weird, as if he didn't know who he was, and so he also embraced this feeling, and admitted to himself: 'Right now I really don't even know who I am!' He could feel deep layers of his own muscles relaxing and giving up.

Then he suddenly saw a caterpillar, a very tired and exhausted caterpillar, a caterpillar who its entire life had been traveling as fast as it could and eating every green thing in sight until it had become so fat that it could hardly take anther step. Caterpillar then crawled along a branch and seemed to melt into one of the branches. Looking more closely David realized it wasn't melting but that something was changing about it. It seemed to be wrapping itself in a blanket. Had he just now thrown a blanket over himself lying here on the couch? The blanket hardened into something light and protective and the caterpillar itself began to melt within that protective shield. Then David realized that the caterpillar itself was melting, getting gooey, fluid, losing the structure that it had known all its life, but it seemed to trust this happening. It abandoned itself to the changes that were taking place within this cocoon. Did it know what it was doing? did it have any sense of what it was turning into? Did it want to change in this way, or did it even have a choice in the matter? David realized that he was lying on the couch in some sort of cocoon, a way of thinking that had become stiff and rigid, and that his logic was trying to hold him while something else melted inside him. Something deep inside was reorganizing itself in a way that David had no control over, and it felt weird, and David felt that he himself was changing but he didn't know how, and he realized that he had become very comfortable in who he had been and he was trying to hang onto that feeling, rather than trusting something very deep within himself and that did know what it was doing even though he had never before experienced such a thing. His entire logical thinking system was reorganizing itself into an entirely new pattern. And then he fell asleep.

The Healing

The lone ship was arriving again in the bay. This time it felt more familiar. David could clearly see the rigging that raised and lowered the great sails. The wooden deck resounded like a drum as he walked upon it. He moved easily over to the yardarm and climbed into the small boat that was being lowered into the sea. The boat hit the sea with a hard crash and he and his fellow sailors began rowing. Rowing was hard, the sea was choppy and seemed to resist the oars, and progress was slow as they rowed toward the shore. They could see the entire village amassed on the shore, carrying weapons, clubs, sticks, and axes of one sort or another. David felt his face and ran his fingers along the three lines on each side of his face. The ridges were prominent and jagged, and a shudder ran through him. But there was also a deep feeling of contentment, of pride, of feeling a warm solid center within his belly. He knew the men, his companions, looked upon him with awe. He felt proud of the scars even thought he knew they disfigured him horribly. They brought both a sense of pride and of disgust.

The men did not want to be on this mission with him. A dread held them together. They felt he was insane but they were also unable to resist his demands. He held a sway over them that they didn't understand, a control that each one felt deep in his own belly. They rowed in unison, he among them rowed harder than any, and slowly the boat inched toward the shore. None of the men felt they would survive. Only Clawface was dead certain.

Arriving close to shore Clawface jumped out of the boat and helped tow it to shallow water. He moved easily toward the amassed people and they parted to let him pass. He walked directly to the man who he had shot and his daughter. Some inexorable power pulled him toward them. Standing before them he put his hands together and bowed toward the father, saying words that neither the father nor his daughter understood, but words they could feel came from deep within this strange man. They understood him to say that he was sorry that he had shot the father and was happy that he had survived. He traced the scars on his face and gestured upward toward the sky, honoring the eagle that had resolved the strange encounter. He put his hands to his heart and then opened them toward the daughter and a wave of warmth and color spread over her face and body.

He listened respectfully as the man replied. His voice was warm and mature, reflecting a deep understanding and a wisdom that surprised Scarface and also thrilled him. The father touched the place on his body that had been wounded and then touched the scars on his face, looking into the sky he waved his hand upward in an arc, connecting their mutual wounds and honoring the great Eagle that had saved them both, and perhaps the entire village, with its strange act.

Both Scarface and the father understood what they were doing, even though neither understood a word that the other spoke. They were participants in a drama that was a link in time, a profound act of presence, and a healing ceremony that had begun with the first hints of life on this earth. They both knew it and yet had no idea of how they knew it. But they also knew it was a ceremony that emanated from the very cells of their bodies. and they both felt there was only one body, and that it was healing itself.

Scared

David awoke with a start. He felt the whole house had shaken him awake. He was sweating and his breath was intense and quick. He instinctively moved his hand to his face to feel the scars but there were none, at least not on the surface. He felt different and totally confused, but the feeling was also good. Something had changed in him but he did not know what. He felt like two parts of himself had grown suddenly together. Two halves of himself that had been strangers, perhaps even enemies, had come together in a profound meeting and had both found a home in him. He was larger, somehow softer but more sure of himself. And he was shaken to his roots as Cornelia spoke.

"You were asleep for a long, long time! I tried to wake you up but I couldn't. You were speaking some strange language and rubbing your face, and there was a strange kind of light around you. It was scary!"

David had not realized she was sitting right in front of him and almost jumped up to run when he heard her voice. He felt shaky and unsure of where he was, or even what year it was, the dream had been so real.

"Why do you look so strange at me? What happened? What were you dreaming about?"

David had no idea how to answer her. Words did not come. He just looked at her and looked at her.

"Now you're really scaring me," she said.

"The future and the past are strangely woven together," he heard himself say, but he was not even sure that it was his voice that spoke. "There is a pattern that binds us all together, and everything in the Universe, and we are also parts of that pattern, as well as its weavers." He did not know where these words were coming from. He had not thought them out before. They were just spilling out of him like water out of a fountain.

He looked gently at this kind girl before him, his little sister, and he knew instinctively that she was not only a part of the pattern but would turn out to be one of its greatest weavers. But he had no idea how he knew this.

A New Place

David said very little during the next few days. He didn't really know what to say, even when someone asked him a question. He didn't know where his thoughts were or what they were, and his feeling was like a bubble or a marshmallow, cushy and soft and indistinct. He experienced the space around himself as if it provided no distinct sense of distance, as if all distance were the same and also as if everything were far far away. But he also realized that every movement he made was tremendously precise and definite. He experienced himself as beyond the law of gravity, and also as if he himself were gravity, and his actions were effortless and also without intent. His entire body felt like a dance only he was not dancing, but the Universe was dancing him.

Cornelia said very little to him but her eyes were always on him, not in any kind of an accusatory way, but watchful and caring, holding him warmly in her gaze without intruding. She understood that he had been through something big and was adjusting to a very new place in himself, like getting to know a new house or a new town. Whenever her mother or father would say something to David, or ask him a question, Cornelia smoothly answered them without even seeming to do so. She surrounded him with a protective cushion of understanding and accountability, and she did it so easily that her protectiveness was hardly noticed by her parents, but David saw and understood what she was doing. There was something in him like a newborn colt trying out its legs for the first time, getting to know the world into which it had been born, and Cornelia was its kindly mother staying near the colt, nudging it from time to time, and being lovingly protective without even seeming to do so.

Mother and Father busied themselves with their usual routines, preoccupied in the same ways they always were, and didn't really notice anything different about David or Cornelia.

And the strange thought occurred to David: 'maybe Cornelia already inhabited that new place that he himself was just now moving into!'

The Flow

Gently, imperceptively, David was emerging from a realm he had never fully understood into a realm that was even larger and where there was not even a question of understanding. Understanding seemed not to be the foundation of this new realm, but could come and go in fleeting swiftness. Understanding was not anything that could support what he was experiencing but seemed to be only one way of thinking and one possibility among many. Something much more deeply present formed the ground upon which he stood, something fundamentally indescribable, yet something that breathed him and participated in the presence that surrounded him like an emanation. He was not alone. There was not even the remote possibility of "alone." He was a dimension of a magical place, although that is not a word he would have used.

He found that language did not even penetrate this realm, although language seemed to spill out of it like a new river gushing out of mountain bedrock. He experienced himself in deep contact with everything around and the self that he felt himself to be was fluid and continuous with this everything. There was no separation nor even the possibility of separation. There was only an ongoing flowing and he was part of it and he was it and it was everything.

"Perhaps poetry is suitable to this realm," he thought to himself, but distinct and definite words were not. They seemed too chunky and separate, like trying to create a river out of bricks instead of water. Words were simply too dense and clumsy even though they were still more present than ever before and he didn't even know their source; they seemed to just appear or evolve in the moment, already fully formed and with a connectedness that was present before they even appeared. They also seemed to be a definite part of aliveness, like fingernails were a part of the body, stiff and functional even though not like the sensitive and pliable skin out of which they grew. Over the next few days David came to respect them more and more. They appeared when needed and disappeared when not in use, and they addressed themselves spontaneously to the needs of the moment. But they were not something he needed to remember or to hang onto. They flowed in and out of situations in their own tempo and David stopped paying attention to them and just trusted them more and more, knowing they would appear when needed and remain silent when not.

Then when he had become fully comfortable with this new realm and this newer David, Cornelia began to tell him about a series of dreams that she had been having.

Dream Visiting

"I didn't want to disturb you," she began, "because I knew you needed your full awareness in that new place."

David was shocked to hear this. She knew! She knew!

"Grandfather has been visiting me in my dreams," she said. "I was surprised at how little he is. And what a funny little beard he has."

David realized for the first time that Cornelia was quite tall for a five year old. David himself had never thought of Grandfather as little, but he now recognized that when they first met David was just a bit shorter than Grandfather. And he had never thought of his beard as funny, but now that Cornelia mentioned it, it was kind of thin and scraggly. But how could she know who a person was that she had never met, but only dreamt about?

"Tell me what happened in your dream!"

"Well, I've been having at least one dream every night since you've been in this strange new place. Grandfather came and he told me that you were in a very important phase of developing, and he showed me the village, and the large wooden hall, and he introduced me to Bearman. I seem to be hanging out in the village with them every night while I'm asleep."

David knew that he had been planning to take Cornelia to the village to meet Grandfather when she got older, so he was astonished to hear about her dreams. Was Grandfather initiating this visit or was it simply a dream of hers growing out of her wishing to know where David had been. But if Grandfather was causing it, why now when she was still so young? And was it possible that one person could visit another in their dreams? David no longer knew what to think.

And suddenly he saw what he was doing! He was trying to understand Cornelia in terms of the things he knew about himself, but what if her own being was completely different from his? What if she had abilities that he knew nothing about? What if she could do things, and know things, and go places that he was unable to? He suddenly realized that he had been trying to fixate her inside of the ideas that he had about himself. And this in itself astonished him. He suddenly recognized that he had frozen himself inside a set of ideas. This was no different than what he had been realizing about Mother and Father, that each was caught in a cage of their own making, having made it of the thoughts they had learned to repeat over and over. And was he any different? Didn't he have his own thought that he believed were true? And hadn't he been trying to see Cornelia in terms of those same thoughts? But this realization in itself seemed to free him!

Then another thought suddenly struck him. If he did not have a system of thoughts as the center of who he was, then what was there?

Surprise

"Grandfather was actually looking for you. I think he felt your presence since it had been your room for so long but it was now mine, so he was kind of surprised to see me. But we had a great talk. I recognized him at once."

David suddenly awoke from his thinking about thoughts. He didn't understand. "Were you awake or were you sleeping?" he asked Cornelia.

"Silly, I was sleeping. You can only travel fast and far in your dreams. I thought you knew that."

"But was it real or was it a dream," David asked, exasperated.

"It was a real dream! Don't you understand?" Cornelia was

also beginning to feel frustrated at David's apparent inability to understand. "Dreams are just a different doorway. Don't you know that?"

"Not in that way. Who taught you that?"

"Who taught you to look through your eyes and to hear through your ears? I just do that naturally. It's how I work. You mean you don't know those things? Do you live in a cage like Mommy and Daddy?" Cornelia didn't know whether David was being deliberately obtuse or if he really did not know. Then she suddenly stopped: "Oh, my! You really don't know, do you?"

David was shocked. He suddenly realized that Cornelia lived in a place that was far different from the place where he lived, yet he had thought it was alike and only slightly different. Could it be that she knew realms that he was only now beginning to discover? Was she born already knowing those realms? Had he known them also and somehow lost his knowing? Or is it possible that every person is born more advanced than those that were born earlier? With abilities that are essentially unknown to older people? Would David even be able to catch up with the place where Cornelia lived? Or would he be trapped in a place that was limited, not unlike the place that his parents occupied in comparison to him?

Or was it possible that parents tried to stunt each new generation so that they would not advance beyond the parents? Was school only a place where people were packaged to look and think like the older generation? And how long had this been going on? A shudder of dread swept through David as he considered what he was just now thinking.

The Teacher?

"I think you know many things that I don't." David said this very slowly to Cornelia. "I knew you have an unusual depth for your age, but now I think that you were born knowing many things that I have only recently been learning in the village, and maybe things that I will never know."

"Maybe that's why Grandfather was asking me so many questions about myself. I thought he had come to ask about you, but we spent most of our time together with him asking me about me. I wanted to know about him and the village and the things he was teaching you there, but he just asked me more and more about me. Of course I was happy to answer his questions but it did seem strange that he was so curious about me. I thought he had come to find out about you and how you were doing at home."

Although David had dreamt occasionally about Grandfather and the village, his dreams had never been about visiting and talking to Grandfather. He wanted to know more, so he asked Cornelia: "How did he first visit you? What happened?"

"Well, I was sleeping and I heard a knock, like someone was knocking at the door. Only I know we have a doorbell, so I thought why would someone be knocking at the door? I opened my eyes and this little funny man was standing in my room. I don't know who was more surprised, me or him. Then I just said, 'Grandfather!' and I saw that he was now really surprised. He acted embarrassed and began to say he was sorry, but I just told him that I had really been looking forward to meeting him, so I was glad he had come. He looked confused and said he had heard my call, and that confused me because I hadn't called him. Then he said he thought it was you that had called him and that's why he had come. Then he seemed to realize I was your sister and his face brightened and he relaxed and smiled. What a gentle smile he has, and such deep eyes; they seem to look right through you. Then I invited him to sit down and we both sat on the floor, only it wasn't in my room but in the big wooden house in the village and I knew I was dreaming. We were sitting on some soft furs. That's when he began to ask me so many questions about myself."

"First he asked me how old I am and when I told him I was five his eyes really opened wide. So I asked him how old he was and he grinned from ear to ear. He said he felt we were equals but he didn't tell me how old he is. How old is he, anyway?"

"I don't know that myself," David answered, curious that he had never asked Grandfather that question, and yet it was one of the first things Cornelia had asked him. "What did you talk about?"

"I wanted him to teach me the way he had taught you, but he just kept asking me question after question, and each time I answered his eyes just seemed to open up even more. I didn't understand what was going on. Was he that way with you?"

"No," said David deep in thought. "He seemed to know all about me already, and we drove directly to the village and then Bearman started teaching me, only it wasn't exactly teaching as much as bringing me into situations where I had to allow my body to meet situations I had never been in before. It wasn't at all like school had been but my body seemed to be really happy to do things it had never done before, and I was delighted to discover that it knew how to do things before I had ever really learned them."

"Now that you say that I recognize that Grandfather was asking questions in order to know how my thinking works and how I know things, but these are things that I didn't learn but just discovered in myself by watching what I do. I also watched Mommy and Daddy and seemed to learn where they would go and where they would seem to stumble when I asked them questions. And there were things that they really didn't want to know. I realized they were very uncomfortable whenever I asked them questions about you and when you would be coming home. They didn't know but they didn't seem to want to ask those questions themselves. And whenever I asked them about their own bodies they always said I was too young to know about that, and they would get red and turn away. I never understood why they didn't want me to know some things. If I could formulate a question why couldn't they formulate an answer," Cornelia asked in complete earnestness.

David could not believe that his little sister could even formulate such a sentence!

"Anyway," Cornelia continued, "suddenly Bearman came into the large room and he was surprised when I said hello to him. It was so great to meet him. I just knew he would take me into the mountains like had taken you. He acted awkward, like he didn't know who I was or what to do, and he started to leave but Grandfather asked him to stay, so he sat down on the floor with us and I started to ask him questions. Both he and Grandfather just stared at me. Then they looked at each other like they couldn't even believe I was there. It was puzzling. Why shouldn't I be there, they were! Of course I didn't mind answering their questions, in fact, I started to see what they were trying to understand about me. They were really curious about why it was so easy for me to be there, and they kept asking questions about who had taught me and where I had learned, and I just kept telling them that no one had taught me, and that I had learned by myself and from myself, and that I thought everyone knew the things that I did but that it seemed that some people wanted to hide what they knew, even to hide it from themselves. I felt like I was teaching them about me rather than them teaching me about them or helping me learn things I didn't know. And then I just woke up in my own bed and felt really grateful that Grandfather had come, and that he had taken me to the village, but I was still puzzled about Bearman not taking me into the mountains to meet the bear. I really would have loved that."

David realized that Cornelia had been thoroughly interviewed by Grandfather, and he felt like Bearman had met a new species of animal that he had never seen before. Was Cornelia in fact a new kind of being that had never before existed? David realized he had many of the questions that Grandfather had been asking Cornelia but he had never asked them directly. Who was the teacher and who was the student?

The Horse

"The next night I fell asleep but I went immediately to the village rather than waiting for Grandfather," Cornelia continued. David couldn't believe his ears.

"I saw where he was sleeping in the big house and so I knocked just as he had when he had come to visit me. He opened his eyes and really looked surprised. I apologized for waking him up but I said I thought he wouldn't mind since we were obviously meant to visit each other. He rubbed his eyes and offered to make some tea for me. He went outside for a little while and when he came back in he had some fresh leaves in his hand and he made a little fire and boiled some water in a clay pot and put the leaves in it. I sat on the floor where we had sat the night before and began to look around."

"I noticed there were other people also sleeping in that big wooden house. I had not noticed them the night before during our first visit. There were clusters of people sleeping together as well as some people sleeping alone. Each person or cluster seemed to have their own amount of space around, and they were also comfortably covered with blankets or furs. There was a soft warm murmur in the room that was very comforting. But no one was awake other than Grandfather and me. But I don't suppose we were really awake, were we. We were both dreaming."

David listened, still astonished that Cornelia could speak so evenly and knowingly about this topic. Traveling and being so aware during dreaming were things only very mature and accomplished people could do, or at least so David thought. He had heard stories of old shamans who could visit each other during their dreams but how could a five year old girl be doing this? And with such assurance and certainty!

"Grandfather gave me a cup of warm tea and we both drank together. It was delicious. I told him he was a good teaman and we both laughed. I asked him how we could visit like this, in our dreams, since I had never done it with anyone else before. He told me he only knew of very old people who could do this and that he had never before been visited by a five year old girl. I thought he was saying this only to make me feel at home but he insisted that what I was doing was unusual. He also told me that he had never before made tea for anyone in his dreams and we both laughed and said it could be our personal ceremony. I told him I would make tea for him the next time he visited me in my home. He really smiles a lot and you can feel the smile beginning deep in his belly before it shows up on his face."

In the five years David had known Grandfather he had always been serious and he had never seen him laugh very much.

"I asked Grandfather if he would teach me like he had taught you. He said that he didn't really know if there was anything I could learn from him. He said he was interested to learn about me and that I seemed to be grownup already even though I was still a small girl. I told him I had always felt like me and that what he was saying didn't make any sense other than the fact that my own parents seemed to be terribly stuck in some strange way that I didn't really understand. I said I hoped I wouldn't get to be like them when I grew up. I told him that you and he were the only grownups that I knew and that I wanted to grow up to be like you. Like both of you. He laughed and said he thought I may have been born already grownup."

"So I asked him about meeting animals, the way you had met Bear and Dolphin. He said that it was not that simple, that the animals also needed to choose to meet me and that he didn't know if any were ready to do that. Then he looked at me really strangely, like he was looking through me but also deeply into me, strange short breaths started coming from his nose, and after a while he said that perhaps there was a horse that was interested in meeting me. I told him that Jennie the giraffe was already a good friend and that maybe she knew the horse. He squinted his eyes at me and then told me to look at the place between my belly and my heart so I looked down at myself but he laughed and said he meant for me to look inside with my feelings rather than with the eyes I used for the outside world. Then I suddenly felt a pounding in the place he meant and I suddenly saw a horse galloping toward me. The horse stopped suddenly when it was right in front of me and it asked me to get on and ride it. I had never ridden a horse before but suddenly I was on its back and it started walking around, and then moving faster and faster. I thought I might fall off but I didn't, in fact staying on its back was really easy. I felt like it was a part of me, like we were both growing out of the same body, and that my legs were really strong and touched the earth easily and powerfully, pounding it really, but as it did there was a lightness in my body, like I was flying easily along the surface of the earth."

"The horse carried me to a lovely little spot that was green and the grass was soft and juicy, and this spot was surrounded by soft trees, and I could hear birds and other little animals in the woods around but I couldn't see them. I got off the horse in this gentle place and I laid down on the soft grass. The horse stretched out beside me with its belly on the grass and it just looked at me with big brown eyes. Its eyes just swallowed me up and I was suddenly with a group of other horses in a different place. I could smell them and it was a good smell, warm and intense, and we began running, galloping, over hills and then faster and faster, and they were all following me, I was in the lead and the faster I ran the faster they followed. Then I slowed down. I could smell fresh water ahead and I walked up to a river that was so clear you could see right through it to the bottom. I went over and drank some water. It was cool and tasted so good. The other horses gathered around me and they all drank too."

"Then I suddenly opened my eyes and I was back in my bed. I felt really good, and it felt like I was bigger and that there were things I knew about being a horse and about being with others. I felt like I had grown bigger and could see more clearly, not with my eyes but with my feelings."

David realized that Grandfather had agreed to become Cornelia's teacher, and Cornelia seemed to understand that also, although neither one spoke about it.

Cornelia's Visit

David did not know what to make of Cornelia's ability to travel and to visit with Grandfather during her dreams, and he was astonished that she took this ability so lightly, as if it were completely natural to be able to do this. And he began to wonder if there were other abilities she had that he did not know about. She was young and she thought that everyone had the same abilities that she had; she didn't know many people other than her parents and David so there was no way for her to judge what was a natural ability and what was exceptional and perhaps even astounding. David was determined to ask Grandfather about her the next time he visited. But when would that be? And hadn't Grandfather come to visit him when he first met Cornelia? Why had Grandfather come? And how would David know when Grandfather was dreaming a visit and when he was physically present? Or had he expected to visit David in one of David's dreams? Or did he have some concern about what David had recently gone through and had come to warn him or to advise him about it? Would it be possible for him to contact Grandfather in a dream just as Cornelia had? Or could he possibly come along with Cornelia the next time she visited Grandfather? He was full of questions but there were no answers. Or at least so it seemed. He exhausted himself wrestling with all these questions and soon fell asleep.

He had not been asleep long when Cornelia entered the guest room and stood by his bedside. He awoke with a start to see her standing beside him. "What's wrong?" he asked.

"Nothing. I was just wondering if I could visit you as well."

"Of course you can! What is wrong?"

"Nothing, I was just wondering if…"

And then it struck David like sudden thunder! Was she visiting him in a dream or were they both awake? And how would he know? Had he ever been really awake other than in the village? Was his entire visit home really a dream? Maybe Cornelia herself was only a dream. What if his entire life was just a long and complicated dream. These thoughts flitted through his mind like so many mosquitos, one after another. He reached out to touch Cornelia but she was gone!

Crazy

The next morning at breakfast David looked imploringly at Cornelia as she and David and Mother and Father sat at the breakfast table, but she seemed either unconcerned or uninterested. He was full of questions for her but he knew he could not speak about dream visits in front of Mother and Father. They would both think he was crazy.

How long had he held thoughts like this? That if he asked the questions that really interested him his parents would think he was crazy. And what did that mean, to be crazy? Did it mean that you asked about things that deeply interested you when others had no interest in them? Did that constitute being crazy? What was crazy, anyway? Was not the ignoring of the obvious crazy? Was not blinding oneself in thought patterns that were repeated over and over again crazy? Was not holding serious judgement about restricting the thoughts of others really crazy? Was not thinking that dreams were unreal to the point of never questioning them really crazy? Was not sitting here in silence while almost bursting with questions crazy? David suddenly realized that perhaps he was doing exactly what his parents did, sitting in silence while thoughts hurried around in his mind but never stating them nor letting them be questioned by others. Wasn't everyone acting the same in itself kind of crazy?

"You seem lost in thought this morning," Mother suddenly said.

David was befuddled. What should he answer? The truth, that he wanted to know if Cornelia had visited him in a dream last night, or if she had actually entered his room and stood by his side. He could feel that Mother would either become concerned about such a statement or else she would try to ignore it, but that she would not seriously consider it as a question. It would disturb her either way. "I was just mulling over a dream I had last night," he finally answered. And how long had he been padding his statements to his parents so that they would not be disturbed out of their own thought cages. Maybe being disturbed was exactly what they needed. But as soon as he thought this he remembered that whenever he had asked something that disturbed them they would then collude with each other, addressing thoughts and questions about David to each other, and making him feel strange and excluded even though he was the center of what was being spoken about. They would agree with each other about what David meant but without ever really addressing David himself. He had felt at those times like he had suddenly become an object, or something that they were together trying to change, rather than a human being in communication with other human beings. He realized that their siding with each other was a way of keeping their thought cages from being disturbed. They colluded in order to keep each other safe, even though safe meant living in a cage made of thoughts and beliefs. And perhaps this was the cage that Grandfather had saved him from even more than the cages that were being built at school. David suddenly wondered to himself what it would be like to visit his old school and his principal. David realized that there was way too much thinking going on and very little communication. Or the communication was remaining inside himself rather than it including others.

Mother and Father both suddenly announced that it was time for them to go to work. They quickly wished Cornelia and David a good day with hopes that they would not be too bored staying at home. David recognized their exit as an obvious escape from an uncomfortable situation. They are hurrying off to a place where their own cages will remain intact, he thought to himself as he wished them also an enjoyable day. He felt somewhat cowardly but also knew that when threatened they would argue their cages back into the place where they felt safe.

Just Doing

"Did you visit me in my room last night or was that only a dream?" he blurted out as soon as his parents had walked out the door.

"Both!" Cornelia answered with a smile.

David was left speechless.

"I wondered if I could visit you the same as I visited Grandfather but you felt so scared that I left before I said anything."

David felt numb but also relieved. The question that he had been bursting with at the breakfast table was answered so simply by his little sister. And it felt so good just to be able to converse freely without having to consider someone else's safeguards.

"I want to learn how to do that. Can you teach me?" he asked.

"I don't know. I just started doing it myself. And I don't really know *how* I do it. It just seems to happen. But I do know that I *really* wanted to meet Grandfather that first time that it did. But Grandfather had really come to see you, it was just that he came to the wrong room. So maybe if you had been in your old room you would have met him at that time in your own dream instead of me."

"But you did come to my room last night in my own dream? Were you dreaming as well or did you really come in? And I really didn't know if I was awake or asleep."

"Yes, that's the way it was when Grandfather first visited me. I didn't know if I was awake or asleep. But last night when I went to bed I really was interested to know if I could visit you in a dream. So maybe really being interested is the preparation."

"Yes," answered David, "and maybe last night I got preoccupied with whether I was awake or dreaming rather than just being present with you when you visited."

"You may be right. When Grandfather appeared in my room *I* was so excited to meet *him* that it didn't matter if it was a dream or not. And when I visited him I was excited about seeing him again. So other questions didn't get in the way. I wonder if questioning and doubting get in the way of knowing," Cornelia suddenly reflected.

David realized what a keen intuitive mind she had, and that *knowing* was more important to her than *how* she knew. Yes, maybe needing to know how gets in the way of knowing. Riding a bicycle is the way I learned to ride, and there is no way I could have known how without doing it. So maybe visiting in a dream is my new bicycle and I just need to do it without first having to know how.

David felt relieved, like he had resolved an old stumbling block. Maybe thinking that he first needed to know how got in the way of actually doing. But wasn't this exactly what Bearman had been teaching him in the village: to just trust being in a situation and that his doing was itself the learning.

And wasn't this exactly the source of the cages that Mother and Father had built? Their knowing really got in the way of just being present!

Teacher Cornelia

David felt greatly relieved following the realization he had just had. It was so simple and yet so profound. His mind had been jumbled up with thinking. He thought he needed to know before doing. And he really just needed to do and to learn from the doing itself. Doing itself was the teacher. He realized he had been getting in the way of his teachers all his life. In fact his parents had been also, and so had his teachers at school. Only

Bearman and Grandfather and the people in the village did not let thinking get in their own way. Not that they didn't think, but that they trusted their doing without having to first think about what they would do, or to think they first needed to know how before they tried something. But this is what he had done in the village. Why was he different now that he was home?

Now he understood that was one of the things that was so different about Cornelia. She trusted her doing and didn't need to think something through before she did it. That's why she was so fresh and enjoyable to be with. She was always directly present in her relationship with David. Her thinking did not get in the way. She could think, and she could think deeply and beautifully, but she did not need to think first. What if thinking was something that was supposed to come after doing rather than before? He suddenly realized that that is the way that thinking had come to encage doing; by insisting on being first. And wasn't this also what he had been being taught at his school up until the time that Grandfather had rescued him?

And was this why grandfather had insisted that it was time for him to come home again? So that he could see how easy it was to revert to the situation, to once again become automatic in the place where that was expected of him? Was this also one of Grandfather and Bearman's lessons? To put him in this situation so that he could learn directly from what he did in this situation? He realized what excellent teachers they were. They didn't try to teach him by telling him, but trusted that he would learn from his own doing and his own awareness by just being in the situation itself.

David also understood why Cornelia was such an excellent teacher for him.

Experiencing

With this realization David was pacified. He could relax now. His mind was no longer ajumble with the desperate need to understand. He breathed deeply now and easily. And breathing seemed to be what he had not been doing. At least not easily. He recognized that his breath had been hard and fast and forced. And the thought came to him: Was breathing like his mind? Like a mirror of his mind?

But then another thought entered: What exactly was understanding? What does understanding mean? What happened when he understood something? And why would his breathing be involved? Was it breathing that understood, or was it his thinking, or was it something deeper? Perhaps something even deeper than himself. But that didn't make any sense. But what does sense mean? David realized that he was getting all caught up in words, and that perhaps understanding was something deeper than words. He realized that when he understood something he felt at home in a situation, that somehow he fit in a way, or that the situation fit himself. It was like putting on clothes that felt comfortable as opposed to putting on clothes that didn't fit. But he also knew that it was not about clothing but about something more like a story, like the story made sense, the story fit or perhaps he himself fit into the story in some way.

And he suddenly realized that in dreaming and needing to know there was a story that he had been telling himself and that Cornelia was telling him things that did not fit into the story that he already knew. Then it struck him. He needed to begin telling himself a story about dreaming that was larger than the story he had been telling himself all his life, a new story where there was room to act within a dream even though he did not know how to do that. And then something opened up within him that was like a zipper opening a jacket that had been too tight.

If the story he told was smaller than his experience he needed to tell a larger story. It was as simple as that. And he knew he had been seeing it all his life. He had constantly been confronted with that when he was with Grandfather and Bearman. And he also saw the cages that his parents were caught in. Their story was too small to allow for more experience and so they excluded

52

new experiences in order to continue to tell the same story. They limited their experiencing to the story they already told, and he had been doing the same now without fully realizing it. A lack of understanding meant that the story he told himself needed to grow bigger. He saw that he had been trying to juggle the old story in order to fit new experiences. But people were in charge of stories. And especially of the stories that they themselves told. The need to tell a consistent story was limiting their ability to take in new experiences.

David had just realized that experiences needed to be the determining limit rather than stories. But did people have an innate need for consistent stories or was it something that each person learned? And wasn't this exactly the difficulty that he had had with the school he had been attending in this small town? The school was based on stories rather than on experiences. And Grandfather and Bearman and now Cornelia had all shown him that their own stories grew to encompass experience. Their stories were flexible and alive. Mother and Father told stories that excluded experiences, and so they were as dead as a repeated story that is too small for aliveness.

Profoundly Present

"Are you ready?"

David was startled almost out of his skin to hear Cornelia's voice. He had thought he was alone in his room, although he realized he had been in deep thought. He looked at her and prepared to answer her when he saw that she held her finger to her lips.

Why does she want me to be quiet? Is someone here? he thought to himself.

Cornelia quietly took David's hand and led him to the door and opened it. They both stepped through. David was still wondering what was going on when he felt like he had been struck by lightening. They were in the large room of the long-house and Grandfather was standing in the middle of the room!

Grandfather quietly invited them to sit down.

"You think too much. That is why I wanted you to go home for a while. Now you are being startled out of your thinking. That is good."

"And I am so happy to have met your little sister. She is little and young, only five years old, but in her awareness she is a giant and she is ancient. You can learn much from her."

David suddenly realized that his own thinking had been brought to a standstill. And it felt good. The struggle was over. He greeted grandfather with deeper thanks than he had ever felt before. Now he really knew what it was to be profoundly present!

A Cup of Tea

"Let's have a cup of tea," Grandfather said.

David saw that the pot of water was already boiling and Grandfather took some fresh herbs and put them in the pot. He brought out a small cup for each of them and when the herbs had steeped enough he poured a cup for each of them, first Cornelia, then David, and last of all for himself. David held the cup in both hands as it had no handle, and in fact, it was more like a small bowl.

"Now that you know you can travel in your dreams we can meet more often and you won't have to wait for me to arrive in my Beetle," Grandfather said to David, with a smile on his lips.

"Why didn't you come to me through a dream the first time you came?" David asked.

"Because we needed to bring your body here as well as your awareness. Your body and your awareness needed to wake up together, and that was Bearman's job. Once they were together then you could begin to learn that they could also be deliberately separate, as they are now. Eventually some very wise people can learn to bring their body along after their awareness has travelled but that usually requires very deep experience that only very old people have had the time to develop. Right now it is important that you learn the flexibility of your awareness and how to go with it to the places where it is needed, or to where it needs to go."

"But if my body is back at home, and my awareness is here, then where am I?" asked David with concern.

"Ah," said Grandfather, "you are your identity, and that began to loosen while you were here with us, but you needed to go back to where that identity first began in order to loosen it fully. Eventually it will learn that it was never supposed to be in charge. It really developed for the sake of other human beings. And it was mainly useful in situations where you needed to survive among other humans who were deeply stuck in their own identities. An animal or a tree or a mountain or the sea needs no identity. It is just who it is and it does what it does, and it doesn't have to account for itself to others, as humans have learned to do. And a craziness has developed among some humans where they think that their identity is more valuable than their awareness, and they spend their entire lives developing an identity rather than loving their aliveness. Aliveness and existence are the true gifts that the Great Universe has given us."

David saw Cornelia nod in agreement. She seemed to be hearing something that she already knew, but for David this was something quite important that he had never fully realized before.

Grandfather saw the opening in David, so he continued. "For some cultures identity begins with being given a name. A name is first of all just a sound, but some sounds have a long history That sound becomes the thing that is made when our attention is desired by someone else, and we quickly learn to focus our attention in the direction from which the sound comes. After a while we begin to make that sound ourselves, and we then think that we are the sound. But a sound is just a sound. In cultures that have remained more in relation to the earth and to nature a child discovers the name that belongs to him, so his identity begins with his own discovery of himself through his experience. Bearman, for example, got his name because as a child he wandered fearlessly into the mountain and a mother bear who had lost a cub began to care for him. He was gone for days and everyone wondered where he was but we could feel that he was all right. He finally wandered back into the village fat and happy but with the smell of bear on him, and he told us that he had found his bear mother in the mountain. She had loved and fed him like a cub and he returns to her whenever he wishes."

"That must be who I met on the mountain! I wondered why Bearman wasn't afraid of it!"

"Bearman has little fear, except where needed. He has always been that way. Some people carry around old fears that they have packaged, but not Bearman. But let me say a little more about identity now that you have asked," added Grandfather with a soft smile.

"The most difficult aspect of identity is that people band together based on identity, and in this mood they lose sight of the fact that we all share this earth, this Universe. No one owns it, no one has the right to restrict another from it, and no one has any right at all to injure anything that exists. We may add to it, we may require aspects of it, but similarly something is also required of us."

David didn't understand what Grandfather was talking about but he knew from previous talks with Grandfather that he usually made sense along the way. He had only to wait and to invite his awareness.

"When people gather around a presumed identity they can turn dangerous without the ability to turn back, like a river that is raging. When they form an identity to which they can mutually belong then they lose perspective of their individual wholeness, and the mass of their power can turn destructive, especially if they presume they are threatened. But many people have already abandoned their wholeness and so the presumed identity gives them a sense of belonging to something greater. If they had retained their wholeness they would know that they always belong to the greater whole, to that which we call the Great Universe."

"What is the Great Universe?" Cornelia asked, and David realized that Grandfather had been talking to her as well.

"The Great Universe is the largest wholeness that exists and you have always been a part of it and have always belonged to it and in it," Grandfather replied. "It knows you are here because it has sent you here. And it is important that you recognize this in everything you do. You may not know why you are here but that is part of the great mystery. And that is a knowing that your own mind may not have access to but the wholeness of your being does, in everything that it does."

Cornelia nodded, and David realized that she was closer to what Grandfather was talking about than he was. But he also recognized that he was trying to know with his mind rather than with the wholeness of his being.

Attack

'I can't listen to another word,' David thought to himself. 'My mind is so jumbled now that I feel like I'll explode if I sit here for one second more!'

At that very moment Cornelia grabbed David by the hand and yanked him so hard he thought he would fall over and hit his head on the floor. He shut his eyes tight anticipating the blow.

And he was almost as shocked when instead he felt a cool wind blowing in his face. "What is happening?" David opened his eyes to discover that he was flying through the air at a tremendous speed. Glancing around in surprise he saw that he was high in the air, and that Cornelia was by his side. And that they were both birds!

Cornelia swooped downward in a large circle and landed next to a lake. David followed close behind and he was shocked to see another large bird flying toward him. The bird looked like it was trying to collide with David and David knew this would be a deadly fight. He spontaneously swung his feet forward and extended his claws fully prepared to do battle with the attacking bird. At the last minute just before they both collided he saw that the attacker had three red stripes on each side of his beak. And then they slammed into each other with a loud splash! David was shocked to find himself underwater. And there was no sign of the attacker. He swam to the surface and saw Cornelia sitting on the bank of the lake laughing and laughing. As he climbed out of the water he realized that the attacking bird had been his own reflection mirrored in the clear lake. Stunned and dripping he crawled over and sat beside Cornelia. She put her head on his arm and said "That was the funniest performance I have ever seen!"

A New Freedom

David awoke in his bed. It was early morning. He didn't know if this had just been a dream or if he had really been dream traveling with Cornelia. He must ask her! But it was still dark and he didn't even remember going to bed. Could this be just another dream? No. He stood up and walked a few steps. He could feel the floor firmly under his bare feet. He breathed deeply. That felt good! He realized that he felt not just good but great. And he was deeply happy. He knew that Cornelia had come to teach him dream traveling, and he had also had a lovely visit with Grandfather. How perfect that he could now visit Grandfather in his dreams, and perhaps even Bearman, although he knew that Bearman was unpredictable so he was unsure of that. But he felt like he had found a new freedom, not only in his dreams but also in himself. And it was obvious to him that Cornelia was his new teacher!

Mother?

At breakfast that morning both of his parents were their usual selves, absorbed in their own thoughts, and actually not wanting to be disturbed in them. David looked inquisitively at Cornelia. She just rubbed her eyes and asked him to pass the orange juice. Mother served them each an egg and then she and Father sat down and they all ate.

"I had a strange dream last night," Cornelia announced.

'Oh, no,' thought David to himself! 'She can't tell about our traveling together!' He glanced at Mother and Father but they were busy eating and hardly paid any attention to Cornelia. Then Mother said. "Oh, I had a strange dream last night as well. I was with a little old Indian man and he made me some tea. What could that possibly mean?" She looked at David and Cornelia and there was briefly a sense of wonder in her eyes but it quickly left and she continued eating absent-mindedly. Cornelia and David glanced at each other.

"Mother, was anyone else at tea with you in your dream?" David asked.

"I think there was someone else there but it was kind of fuzzy, and I never do remember my dreams. But there was a special feeling in this one, kind of like a mystery or something. Yes, I think there may have been one or two other people there, but it was very fuzzy." She didn't look at her children as she said this and remained focused on her breakfast.

David was dying to ask her more about her dream but he realized she was not wanting to elaborate, nor did she take the dream seriously other than her brief flash of curiosity.

"Anyway," she said abruptly, "it's time for me to be on my way to work, and you also Dear," as she turned to Father.

David recognized this withdrawal. It was such a standard part of her repertoire when she didn't want to explore more deeply. She was safe on the surface and in her own cage. David could almost see a "Do Not Disturb" sign hung around her neck. The cage was a safe place even though she had constructed it herself.

Dreaming Mother?

Cornelia and David just sat and stared at each other after Mother and Father had left for work.

"Did you...."

"No... yes... what?"

Both were trying to speak at the same time. Then they both just laughed.

"Did you see Mother at the meeting with Grandfather?" David asked. He realized he was too surprised at Mother's dream to even ask what he had intended to: whether Cornelia had taken him to Grandfathers.

"No, I thought it was just you and me with Grandfather," Cornelia answered. "How did she get there? Or maybe it wasn't really Grandfather but just a dream she had on her own?"

"But it did sound like Grandfather. And did you take me there or did I take you?"

"I don't know. Could it be that Grandfather just called us both? Did he pull us there or did we go?"

Neither Cornelia nor David seemed to know what had really happened. But they both felt that they could ask Grandfather and that he would know the answers.

Finally David said, "I thought you had taken me there."

"No, it wasn't my doing," Cornelia replied. "Could it be that we each just went independently and met there?"

"I suppose it's possible, but what is this about Mother? Is she visiting with Grandfather as well? Should we talk to her more about her dream?"

"I think she was a bit afraid of talking about it more, but perhaps that was just because Father was present. You know, he does have a dampening effect on Mother's communication. She's much more open with me when he isn't around. When he's present she always acts as if she's afraid he will criticize her."

"Yes, I remember that about them."

Real Journeys

David and Cornelia spent a restless day. They were both eager to make a dream journey to Grandfather and they also wanted to talk to Mother, but they couldn't dream without being asleep and Mother was away at work. They were full of questions together but neither of them knew the answers. They were just restless, stewing in their own questions, knowing their questions were very similar. They were so charged with energy that they decided to go for a walk. They began walking along the street and soon came to a park. Walking along one of the park lanes they suddenly began to run, both at the same time, and they ran together, not in competition to see who could run fastest, but running comfortably side by side, until they came to a grove of trees. A brook ran through the grove and they ran along the brook until it led to a small lake. They both stopped at the same time and sat down on a grassy spot on the bank of the lake.

David suddenly looked at Cornelia and said, "I know what we can do! We can talk to Elephant. I haven't visited Elephant in many years."

"And I could talk to Jessie! I haven't talked to Jessie since you came home!"

"You mean you can talk to Jessie even when she's not here?" asked David.

"Why not? You talk to Elephant even though Elephant isn't here, not really, not like Jessie."

David and Cornelia lay back on the grass and closed their eyes. David silently called out: "Elephant are you here? Could you come visit with me?"

And Cornelia silently said, "Jessie? I know you're really at home on my bed, but could you come visit me here anyway?"

Elephant slowly walked up and said, "I've brought a friend with me." David looked behind elephant and was startled. It was Jessie the Giraffe. He had never visited with her before except for that first time when Cornelia introduced her to David and David had asked Cornelia if she spoke. Then Elephant said, "and I've got another surprise for you as well." David was really shocked now, for here was Cornelia walking along behind Jessie.

70

"Cornelia! Are you really here?"

"I'm just as surprised as you are. I didn't expect to meet Elephant but I certainly didn't expect to meet you also. Is this really happening?"

At this point Elephant and Jessie intervened and said, "Yes, we're all here together. We are used to being wherever we are, it's never a surprise to us, but you two seem to have some fixed rules about what can happen when you close your eyes, just as you seemed to be a bit frozen about who you can visit in your dreams. An inner journey is not that different from a dream journey, and it seems that you are both ready to learn more about this dimension of reality. Reality isn't only outside of you, it's also inside. And you've both just begun to explore this side of what is real."

The Inner Reality

"The Inner Reality is actually much larger than the outer Reality," Elephant began, "and for thousand of years people visited it regularly. They drew most of their wisdom and knowing from it and they trusted it's guidance. They visited each other and also those who had already left them in this Inner Reality. The Inner Reality has a glue that held them together in a very deep and wonderful way. But this was a time when people wandered around freely in small tribes and had many adventures as well in the Outer Reality."

"But when people stopped wandering and began to build towns and cities and lived without taking long walks together they began to have ideas that everybody's Inner Reality should be the same, and they argued about it rather than respecting that every person has a unique experience in their Inner Reality. They began to think that Inner Reality should be as consistent as Outer Reality. This was their great mistake, for then the inner richness of every person began to be eroded, worn down, compared and argued about. And occasionally a strong leader would appear in a city or town who would insist that there was only one Inner Reality and that everyone should see the same thing in it. This was the greatest assault ever upon the most creative roots of the individual person. You see, this began to destroy the very glue that held people together and that enriched the entire community. The Outer Reality held people together only when there was danger or when people were in need and had to cooperate in order that everyone would be fed and could survive. But the Inner Reality was the source of each person's gifts and when they were properly shared with each other there was tremendous abundance in the community."

"These were times when ignorance and control were rampant and people were ejected from the community when their Inner Reality didn't conform to that of the leaders, and later they were even tortured or killed. The leaders justified all of this in their own small minds, minds that had become severely twisted and damaged. People were never meant to control each other but to cooperate and enjoy their time together."

"As time went on people arrived at a place where they were afraid to share their Inner Reality, as you well know, David, and so they kept it hidden, and some even denied that it existed, or became afraid of it when it showed itself. So that even small children were taught that it was not real, and that it was even shameful to carry it or to share it, and so they hid it from others, and some hid it so deeply that it was even hidden from themselves. The greatest source of richness in the world was closed down and it was replaced with people's control of each other."

David was aghast to hear this. Cornelia just listened with intense interest.

"You and Gordy helped me to remain true to my Inner Reality, didn't you Elephant?" exclaimed David.

"Yes," Elephant replied, "we were your lifeline, as well as the council of animals. What you also learned in the village was that there are ceremonies that keep some people connected to their Inner Reality."

Deep Love

Cornelia could not contain herself. She had been itching to say something and finally asked, "Elephant, can I talk to you as well as to Jessie, even though you are David's?"

Elephant laughed a trumpeting laugh. "We don't belong to people even though we have a tendency to visit some people regularly. And there are those who get the idea that we belong to them, but that is only because it has been so long since people have really had a deep intimacy with themselves or with anyone else, and so it is essential that they understand that intimacy and commitment are really possible. They need to learn that commitment and deep relationship are essential in this Universe, and that this is one of the elements that is so necessary to themselves. There is a foundational reality within everyone and if the only knowledge of it they have is in the Outer Reality then they never really understand what being alive is. The kind of relationship a person has with themselves is then what shows up with others in the Outer Reality. Well, actually, there is only one Reality, and it exists in layers, but unfortunately people have become distanced from the deepest layers of who they are. So consistency and deep intimacy are things that need to be reawakened in people and this reawakening is one of our most important jobs."

Cornelia was overwhelmed to hear this. David thought that perhaps she was too young to understand but she understood perfectly. "I used to feel this with Mommy and Daddy," she blurted out, "but that was long ago and I have missed it greatly. Now I know that's what I get from Jessie."

"Yes," Jessie replied, "there always has been a deep love between us."

"I know, I know," Cornelia repeated, "and when I first heard about Elephant and Grandfather I also felt a deep love for them even though I had never met them, but I felt that I already knew them, and that I had known them all my life. And I was so happy to feel that because I had really come to miss it with Mommy and Daddy."

Jessie answered, "Unfortunately Mommy and Daddy had already created a distance from that place in themselves, and even though they also missed that closeness they didn't realize that the distance was inside of themselves, a remoteness from the deepest layer of knowing themselves."

"So do we visit people in our dreams because those are the people that we are closest to?" Cornelia asked. "Like David and Grandfather?"

"Those are the people that it is easiest to visit because they are in deep contact with themselves. And being in deep connection with who they are they also pay attention to their dreams in a deeper way. Your mother and father are already at a great distance from their dreams and this shows up in their relationships with other people as well. And in their connection with animals!"

The Disconnect

When Mother arrived Cornelia could not contain herself.

"We know the little old Indian man that you visited in your dream, Mommy! David and I have also visited him. Isn't he great?"

Mother's face turned ashen white. Her mouth opened but

no words came out. Her eyes were wide open, she looked like she had seen a ghost.

David realized she was in a state of shock. And he also realized that Cornelia, for all her natural brilliance, had not foreseen that such a statement would terrify their mother. She was not at home with her inner reality, other than to treat it as some "thing" that was quite alien. So for such a statement to be made, as if other people knew something about her inner world, brought her to the edge of the defense system that she had set up so long ago.

Mother sat down on a chair and David offered her a glass of water. She took it and drank the entire glassful without stopping.

"Mother, are you all right?"

She looked at him as if she didn't understand his words.

"It is such a warm day, Mother, you must be exhausted. Would you like another glass?"

Again Mother looked at him without a hint of comprehension. He put his hand gently on her shoulder and she let out a start: "David, what are you doing here?"

David hardly knew how to answer her. Had she disconnected from the fact that he had returned home? Did she think she was somewhere else? "You must be tired, Mother, would you like to lay down a while and Cornelia and I will prepare dinner?"

Mother looked around slowly and then focused on Cornelia. "I am awfully tired, I do think I'll lay down a while." She stood up and went into her bedroom.

David and Cornelia just looked at each other in wonder, then David said, "There may be things she's not ready to talk about. Maybe they don't fit into the map of her life. We need to be gentle with her and to approach this slowly. We had a glimpse of a doorway this morning and now it seems it has slammed shut. but maybe it will show itself again. If she is ready to grow it will."

Cornelia just nodded.

Collusion

When Father arrived home from work he was surprised to find David and Cornelia in the kitchen preparing dinner.

"Where's Mother?" he asked.

"She was very tired, Daddy, so she lay down and we offered to fix dinner."

Father just looked at them.

David was preparing some salmon that he had found in the freezer. While in the village he had learned to prepare all the various foods that were available there, and salmon was one of them as well as many different kinds of seafoods and seaweed and roots and berries. The kitchen smelled delicious.

"I didn't know you could cook. Is that one of the things you learned at your special school? It does smell good."

"Yes, Father. Every student learned to prepare various kinds of foods. We learned to be self sufficient in every situation. Sit down. Cornelia, why don't you go call Mother."

Cornelia looked briefly at David with a question in her eye. "Just tell her Father is home and dinner is ready." Cornelia left the kitchen and returned a short while later.

"She said she'd be right here. She said she was surprised. She didn't realize she had been asleep so long. She said she must have been very tired." Cornelia looked knowingly at David.

Father continued his conversation with David. "I didn't know boys learned how to cook at school. We certainly didn't when I was in school. What else did you learn there?"

Just then Mother entered the kitchen. She looked rested and refreshed. "It is so nice to have children that can cook." She sat down at the table. David served her first. "That salmon smells delicious. Is that a maple syrup glaze on it? Wherever did you learn to cook like this?"

"I was just asking him the same thing," Father interspersed. "He says they taught him how to cook at the special school that he attended. I was never taught how to cook at school. But this is mighty tasty. You do a glazed salmon sometimes too, don't you Mother?"

"Yes, I've always enjoyed cooking. Why just last night on the TV they made the most interesting salad. You saw that too, didn't you Dear."

"I did catch a glimpse of it, yes. Well, David, I guess now you and Mother can teach Cornelia how to cook. I bet you'd like to learn to cook like this, wouldn't you, Corny."

"Oh, she's much too young for that, aren't you, Cornelia."

Cornelia recognized that all this talk was really camoflage. She really wanted to talk about her mother's dream, and why Mother had been so dumbstruck when Cornelia had first asked her about it. She realized that Father was helping her avoid it, and she recognized that this happened quite often. Collusion was one of their main defense systems. She felt so thankful that she now had David that she could talk to about things like this because she knew that if she even raised the topic both her mother and father would deny any collusion and claim they were just talking, and that Cornelia must be imagining things. She also recognized that it was difficult to talk to anyone about anything when their first reaction was to deny the reality of the questioner.

The Question

Dinner continued in the same vein, of talking about how good the food was, and about the things a person learned in school, and how nice it would be when Cornelia goes to school. Cornelia felt it was like watching the surface of a deep sea, and she was yearning to dive into it to see how deep the ocean is and what lies at the bottom, but she also understood that her parents dreaded going deeper and that their usual realm was the surface of things. She understood that what she loved about David and also about Grandfather was that she could ask them anything and they would take her questions as valid rather than disqualifying the question and the questioner. She realized that she felt dismissed by people when they thought her questions were "cute," or that she had a vivid imagination, or that she spoke of imaginary things that they didn't consider "real." She suddenly understood that the division between real and not real, or between real and imaginary, was a protective wall that people had built and that it's purpose was twofold, to split awareness in two and also to protect themselves on one side of the wall. The other side of the wall was dismissed before it was given any consideration. But she also suddenly recognized that to dismiss the imaginary half of reality was to dismiss her own questions, and therefore her own value. She also understood that most people did not like to be "wrong," and that the wall was a protection between right and wrong.

As the dinner conversation continued Cornelia realized that she was seeing the depths of the ocean just in how people stayed on the surface. She recognized that David was staying on the surface with their parents as a way to humor them but perhaps also to help protect them from being confronted with the division that they themselves maintained. They did not really want to see their own boundaries, their own structures, and if confronted they would deny that they had any boundaries or that there was a habitual structure, a pattern, that they were very unwilling to look at.

'No one likes to be a pattern,' Cornelia thought to herself, 'they like to think of themselves as alive and as free. Alive and free was part of the story they had learned to tell about themselves and the division in what they allowed themselves to think and to talk about served also to protect the story they told about who they were. It must not be easy to question oneself, because then you must step outside of the story you tell about who you are, and you don't even know where the questioner is standing.' Cornelia was deep in thought when she realized that a question had been put to her by Mother. She looked at her mother and asked, 'What?"

"I asked if you and David had had an enjoyable day, since I was so tired when I arrived that we haven't had a chance to talk."

Cornelia decided to risk it. "Don't you remember, Mom, when you arrived I asked you about the dream you had about the little old Indian."

"I certainly don't know what you're referring to. I haven't had any dream about an Indian. And I went directly to bed when I arrived, I was so tired from working all day, and this is the very first chance we have had a chance to talk. Wherever did you get that silly idea about a dream?"

Cornelia was flustered, but she recognized her reaction, and understood that being flustered was playing into her mother's denial of what had happened. But what could she do? If she tried to confront her mother, and she was very willing to do that, she knew that her mother would just intensify her denial. So she turned to David: "David, you remember our conversation with Mom when she arrived home from work and I asked her about her dream with the old Indian."

Mother and Father were suddenly stock still and all looked at David waiting for his answer. David realized that if he answered truthfully Mother and Father would join together in opposition to him and Cornelia. But he also recognized that mother was in a very fragile position, and that she could easily repeat the reaction that she had when she first arrived and become frozen and tired again, yet he felt an inherent need to validate Cornelia's question and the reality of what had taken place. It was an uncomfortable position to be in.

He turned first to his mother. "Mother, you were so tired when you arrived that I doubt if you remember anything that was said to you at that time." (For this was true right now.) "Cornelia and I had been talking about the reality of dreams and how sometimes they coincide with other things that we have known, and we spoke of the fact that we have both had dreams in which an old Indian man was present."

Then turning to his sister. "Cornelia, I think perhaps we just need to ask our dreams for an answer to our questions, since they are about dreams in the first place."

Cornelia recognized that David was trying to smooth over the situation without confronting their mother, and she understood his subtle statement to her, that perhaps the answer did lie in their dreams themselves. They could both journey tonight to Grandfather and ask him if he had been in one of Mother's dreams, and if so, why Mother was so afraid now. But she knew she would have to talk to David later for she found the present situation untenable.

"David, I think that is a capital idea!"

Again, David was awed at her powerful and skillful use of language.

The Approach

After dinner, while Mother and Father were both watching TV and David and Cornelia were washing the dishes, Cornelia said: "I know you tried to defuse an uncomfortable situation, but I think Mom needs to take responsibility for what she said and did."

"I think so also," David replied, "but I don't think the dinner table was the right place for that. And I felt she would just go into that place of tired withdrawal again, and that Father would get upset and blame us for it. She is at a very delicate place in her balance. On the one hand we know about her dream because she told us, and on the other she seems to be terrified of it and would rather disappear than to be confronted about it. It is the ultimate place of retreat, and I think Father would have tried to support her and be against us, and that would create a very difficult rift. You know he frequently moves to a position of opposition, but this time it would be him and Mother against you and me."

"So, how should we go about it then?"

"I think the best approach is to visit Grandfather together tonight and to ask his advice."

"Good, that sounds exciting!"

The Longhouse

It was nighttime, and the longhouse was quiet except for the gentle snores and warm murmurs of people sleeping. Grandfather was waiting and the water for tea was already boiling.

"Hello, welcome, I have been expecting you. Sit here with me and we'll have a cup of tea." He poured the boiling water over the fresh herbs and handed a small bowl of it to each of his guests. They each greeted Grandfather warmly and took the bowl in both hands, feeling its gentle warmth suffusing into their hands and letting it cool before sipping. Grandfather held his also and looked deeply at each of them but in a very unobtrusive way, seemingly shy but very present. Profoundly present. His guests each felt a gently tangible acceptance, not just of their own presence but throughout the depth of their being, an acceptance without judgement of any sort, held by grandfather's presence while they arrived and relaxed, layer by layer.

"Grandfather, did you…"

"Were you with…"

Both eagerly spoke at the same time, then stopped together, looked at one another, then at Grandfather, and they all laughed.

"You seem to be in a hurry. Just feel the energy of that need and give it some room in who you are."

Each breathed deep and long, took yet another breath, and then sipped the tea.

"Allowing hot tea to cool is a very good way to arrive. This hot tea is a gift of the earth, of the water, of the herbs, and of the fire, and we join together with the earth and all of her gifts as we imbibe it together. The earth is seldom in a hurry, and yet accomplishes so very much at her own natural pace. People in a hurry frequently trip over their own feet." Grandfather's settledness infused itself into his guests as the tea filled their bellies and the warmth their bodies.

Finally Cornelia spoke. "We need to know if you visited Mommy in a dream."

"Why not ask her yourself, she is sitting here with you."

David and Cornelia almost jumped out of their skins. They had been so focused on Grandfather and on the questions that were jumping around inside of them that they had not noticed Mother sitting to their left, comfortably sipping her tea.

"Mother..."

"Mommy..."

Again both stopped, looked at one another, and laughed. Grandfather also had a smile on his lips and their mother sat demurely present.

"Mother, how long have you been visiting Grandfather?"

"I don't really know. Recently, as I sleep, I am suddenly here with him. We don't have much to say to each other but it feels so very good just to be here. I don't really know the man but being here with him fills me with such a sense of satisfaction. And it feels so natural for both of you to be here as well, and I don't seem to have any questions, in fact I don't even think much when I'm here, I just relish the beauty of a place deep inside. It's a place that I remember having when I was a girl, a place where everything is so natural and easy, and there is no requirement to perform in any particular way."

David and Cornelia sat in stunned silence. They had never heard their mother speak in such an easy and relaxed manner before. This seemed like a woman that they had never really known before now, yet they both knew her in her own somewhat frantic and obedient way at home.

"Your mother has room here but only when she is deeply asleep. When she is awake she steps into that self that she learned to be for the sake of others, to serve, to perform, to attend to other people. And the basis of her performance is a fear, a fear of not being accepted, fear of being rejected, of being judged as not good enough, and that layer of fear is the thing that holds her together as the mother both of you have known. This is your mother deep inside of who she is, but her fear holds her into two parts, and in order for her to heal back into one being she will have to go through the experience of that fear when she is awake. She cannot be shoved through it, that would just increase the fear, but if she is loved and treated gently she may eventually be able to heal together these two sides of who she is."

David and Cornelia stared in utter silence as Grandfather spoke. This is not at all what they had been expecting.

The Roots

"Yesterday when I asked her about her dream she almost fainted and then later acted as if she had just been tired. How can we help her to heal from this fear?"

"To ask her about this side of herself would throw her into a panic, fainting is the sudden retreat from the panic. Instead of asking her about her dreams, just tell her about your own.

Not abruptly, not forcefully, but gently and almost as an aside. Let her hear how at home you are with your own dreams, how intriguing you find them, how curious you are about them. But also how you recognize them as a deep aspect of who you are."

"Dreams are the roots of our reality in the existence of the Universe, and this Universe nurtures us through them and promotes our growing and our union with the greater whole. Dreams seem strange because the reality out of which we grow is itself strange when compared to our daily life. Our daily life is like the blossom standing in the sunshine and sharing itself with the bees and the butterflies, but the blossom knows almost nothing of the roots that are buried in the dark and moist earth, and how those roots embrace their darkness and earthiness in order to nurture the growing that eventually results in the blossom. The blossom reaches for the sunshine. It has to. That is its job. But the roots reach for the depth of the earth, and there it is dark and moist and very close."

"The blossom needs space around itself, but the roots need the contact with the inside of the earth and the gentle pressure that holds them there. the blossom is not the roots and the roots are not the blossom, but they are always in close relationship with each other, necessarily so. And so in this way they participate in each other's existence, although they are almost polar opposites. But they do have an almost magical and essential relationship. Each would die without the other, however the roots can grow for a long time without appearing above the earth as the shoot that eventually blossoms. There can be no blossoming without the roots, but the roots can exist for a long time without giving rise to a blossom. The roots must wait for a certain conjunction, a specific alignment of season and weather and moisture and soil before it dares poke its head above the ground. The roots themselves must be in alignment with the rest of the Universe before they can make the jump necessary for aliveness to show its lovely face. We don't know how lucky we are that our own roots have dared trust the present circumstances. Of course we are different from the flower, much more complex, and so strongly committed to asking questions about our own existence."

"So respect your dreams and realize that the blossom can only be what it is because of the commitment of the roots, and that the flower must accept the mysterious differences. Understanding does not need to be in control but it can still honor its own mysterious roots."

Cornelia did not understand, and neither did David, but they both felt an awesome and deep respect for the mysterious complexity of their own existence. And they had a renewed respect for the dreams that intrigued them so.

The End.

Stories for the Inner Child
Series Information

Dream Visits is volume 3 of the series "Stories for the Inner Child," a series of novels by Steve Gallegos that explores living with the Deep Imagination as a vital and alive part of human awareness.

Stories for the Inner Child Series:
Nothing is Nothing, Book 1 ISBN-10 0-944164-24-2
by Steve Gallegos (E.S. Gallegos Ph.D.), 2013

Something is Something, Book 2 ISBN-13: 978-0-944164-28-0
by Steve Gallegos (E.S. Gallegos Ph.D.), 2014

Dream Visits, Book 3, ISBN-13: 978-0-944164-30-3
by Steve Gallegos (E.S. Gallegos Ph.D.), 2015

Forthcoming titles
Mother, Book 4
by Steve Gallegos (E.S. Gallegos Ph.D.), *coming December 2015*

Father, Book 5
by Steve Gallegos (E.S. Gallegos Ph.D.)

Bearman, Book 6
by Steve Gallegos (E.S. Gallegos Ph.D.)

Grandfather, Book 7
by Steve Gallegos (E.S. Gallegos Ph.D.)

About the Author

Eligio Stephen Gallegos (aka Steve) was born the state of New Mexico in the southwestern United States in 1934. Of Native American, English and Irish descent, Steve was raised in the local Hispanic culture speaking both English and Spanish. A gifted craftsman he was involved in woodcarving, leatherwork, silverwork, and drawing and painting from an early age and greatly disliked the confinement and regimentation of school even though he was a intellectually gifted student.

After military service, he completed his undergraduate work at the University of Wisconsin, his masters at New Mexico State and his Ph.D. in Psychology at Florida State University. He taught at Mercer University, Macon, Georgia between 1967-1981. After fourteen years as professor of psychology in Macon, GA, Steve undertook a residency in psychotherapy in the State of Oregon and became a practicing psychotherapist.

While in Oregon, Steve underwent a spiritual experience that changed him profoundly. This experience is described in The Personal Totem Pole Process (ISBN 9780944164099). He describes the experience as *"spontaneously meeting the alivenesses that were rooted in my energy centers and that presented themselves primarily as animals, but they had to be approached through the knowing of the deep imagination. I realized that the teacher I had sought for my entire life was in fact deep within my imagination and had always been there."*

Since then, introducing people to their own inner animals and the rediscovery of the wisdom of the imagination, has been his path in life. For over 30 years, he has taught people how to access their wholeness through developing a relationship with their deep imagination. Steve discovered and developed the Personal Totem Pole Process® as a way of meeting the inner animals and beings of the deep imagination.

Through his books and writings, he has explored many healing aspects of the deep imagination. He holds that one of our major challenges is to return to balance between the ways of knowing, so that Thinking, Sensing, Feeling and Imagery are once again fully available to each of us, both for our own grow-ing and the world's wholeness.

At present he is primarily engaged in offering workshops and in training others in the exploration of the deep imagination in the United States, Ireland, Germany, Austria, France, Den-mark, the Czech Republic, Macedonia, Portugal, and Australia.

For further information on trainings, workshops and individual sessions using the Personal Totempole Process© and Deep Imagery, please contact Steve:

www.esgallegos.com   info@esgallegos.com

Resources

For information on Deep Imagery:

International Institute for Visualization Research
PO Box 632
Velarde NM 87582
www.deepimagery.org
www.facebook.com/deepimagery
IIVR@deepimagery.org

Eligio Stephen Gallegos, PhD,
PO Box 468
Velarde NM 87572
www.esgallegos.com
info@esgallegos.com

BOOKS ON DEEP IMAGERY FROM MOON BEAR PRESS:

Control and Obedience: The Human Illness
by E.S. Gallegos Ph.D. (2016)

Chakra Power Animals: The Living Energies of the Chakras
by E.S. Gallegos Ph.D. (2016)

The Personal Totempole Process: Animal Imagery, the Chakras and Psychotherapy
by E.S. Gallegos Ph.D. Kindle Edition (2012)

Animals of The Four Windows:
Integrating Thinking, Sensing, Feeling and Imagery
by E.S. Gallegos Ph.D. ISBN: 0944164404

Into Wholeness: The Path of Deep Imagery
by E.S. Gallegos Ph.D. ISBN 978-0944164228

Little Ed and Golden Bear
by E.S. Gallegos Ph.D. ISBN 978-0944164068

The Circus Cage: A Journey of Transformation
by Rosalie G. Douglas. ISBN 978-0944164020

www.ingramcontent.com/pod-product-compliance
Lightning Source LLC
Chambersburg PA
CBHW070501130626
46555CB00003B/1099